Crinkleroot's Guide to GIVING BACK TO NATURE

By Jim Arnosky

G. P. PUTNAM'S SONS • An Imprint of Penguin Group (USA) Inc.

To Bob and Anne

G. P. PUTNAM'S SONS

A division of Penguin Young Readers Group.

Published by The Penguin Group.

Penguin Group (USA) Inc., 375 Hudson Street, New York, NY 10014, U.S.A.

Penguin Group (Canada), 90 Eglinton Avenue East, Suite 700, Toronto, Ontario M4P 2Y3, Canada

(a division of Pearson Penguin Canada Inc.).

Penguin Books Ltd, 80 Strand, London WC2R 0RL, England.

Penguin Ireland, 25 St. Stephen's Green, Dublin 2, Ireland (a division of Penguin Books Ltd.).

Penguin Group (Australia), 250 Camberwell Road, Camberwell, Victoria 3124, Australia

(a division of Pearson Australia Group Pty Ltd).

Penguin Books India Pvt Ltd, 11 Community Centre, Panchsheel Park, New Delhi - 110 017, India.

Penguin Group (NZ), 67 Apollo Drive, Rosedale, Auckland 0632, New Zealand

(a division of Pearson New Zealand Ltd).

Penguin Books (South Africa) (Pty) Ltd, 24 Sturdee Avenue, Rosebank, Johannesburg 2196, South Africa.

Penguin Books Ltd, Registered Offices: 80 Strand, London WC2R 0RL, England.

Published simultaneously in Canada.

Manufactured in China by South China Printing Co. Ltd.

Text set in Adobe Caslon Semi Bold.

The art was created with Micron pens and colored with acrylic washes.

Library of Congress Cataloging-in-Publication Data is available upon request.

ISBN 978-0-399-25520-5

1 3 5 7 9 10 8 6 4 2

The activities suggested in this book are things children can do on their own or with some adult supervision. Grown-up conservation measures, such as driving fuel-efficient vehicles, insulating your home, buying locally grown foods, and starting up recycling centers are not included.

—*Jim Arnosky*

H ello! My name is Crinkleroot. I was born in a tree and raised by bees. I live deep in the forest. In the peace and quiet of winter, I think about the trees, the earth beneath the snow, the water under the ice, and the wild animals. I celebrate all these things by giving back to Nature each and every day.

What can just one person do to give back to the Earth? What can someone small like me give back to the sea? I'll show you things I've done throughout the year. Then you can see how you can give something back to Nature, too.

Sometimes giving back to Nature means helping provide food when an animal is hungry. Feeding seeds and corn to wildlife is a great way to help birds that do not migrate and small animals that do not hibernate survive the cold winter.

CAN YOU IDENTIFY THE WINTER BIRDS ON THE NEXT PAGE?
[ANSWERS ON PAGE 48]

Different seeds attract different birds. For instance, chickadees, blue jays, and grosbeaks all prefer sunflower seeds. Squirrels, chipmunks, and mice do as well.

If you mix sunflower seeds in peanut butter and smear it on a tree trunk, woodpeckers will also come to dinner.

Pigeons, sparrows, and juncos like smaller seeds, such as millet. Finches love thistle seeds. And safflower seeds will coax shy cardinals to your feeder.

Whole kernels or cracked corn (dry kernels smashed with a rolling pin) will bring crows and wild turkeys to your yard. And dried corn on the cob will be eaten at night by deer, opossums, and raccoons.

SUNFLOWER SEED

MILLET

THISTLE SEED

CRACKED CORN

SAFFLOWER SEED

WHOLE CORN KERNELS

DRIED CORN ON THE COB

This mound of snow isn't really
snow at all. It's just snow covering a
knoll where I planted grass last fall.

That's what I'm giving to the deer and rabbits living here:
a new green spot to graze this coming year.

TO PLANT GRASS : RAKE TO LOOSEN SOIL · SCATTER SEED · RAKE TO COVER

Let a corner of your lawn grow wild.
It will become a cool and shady tangle
of weeds and tall grass for small
animals to rest, nest, and hide in.

In this patch of lawn grown wild,
I see 2 sparrows, 1 bird's nest with
3 eggs, 2 caterpillars, 7 butterflies,
4 bees, 1 spider and web,
1 snail, 1 grasshopper,
1 chipmunk, 1 mouse,
1 fawn, 1 pheasant,
1 rabbit, and
1 garter snake!

Can you find them all?

Plant a butterfly bush at home or at school. Butterflies feed on the sweet liquid called nectar that is produced inside certain types of flowers. A butterfly bush's flowers will provide nectar from spring to fall.

Each butterfly bush flower plume has hundreds of tiny blossoms, each containing a drop of nectar.

VICEROY

MONARCH

RED ADMIRAL

TIGER
SWALLOWTAIL

ZEBRA
LONGWING

DOGFACE

BLUE

SULPHUR

Here is a sampling
of the butterflies your
blooming butterfly bush
might attract.

By planting nectar-producing flowers, you'll also be providing nectar for hummingbirds. Like butterflies, hummingbirds feed exclusively on flower nectar.

If you live in a place where migrating hummingbirds show up in early spring, you can welcome them with a feeder full of sweetened water. This will give them nourishment until the spring flowers bloom and produce nectar.

To make sweetened water:
mix in ¼ cup of sugar for every
1 cup of water.

East of the Mississippi
River, there is only one species of
hummingbird—the ruby-throated
hummingbird. The female ruby-
throated birds do not have the colorful
throat patch that the males do.

West of the Mississippi River, there is a variety of
hummingbirds. Here is a small sampling to look for.

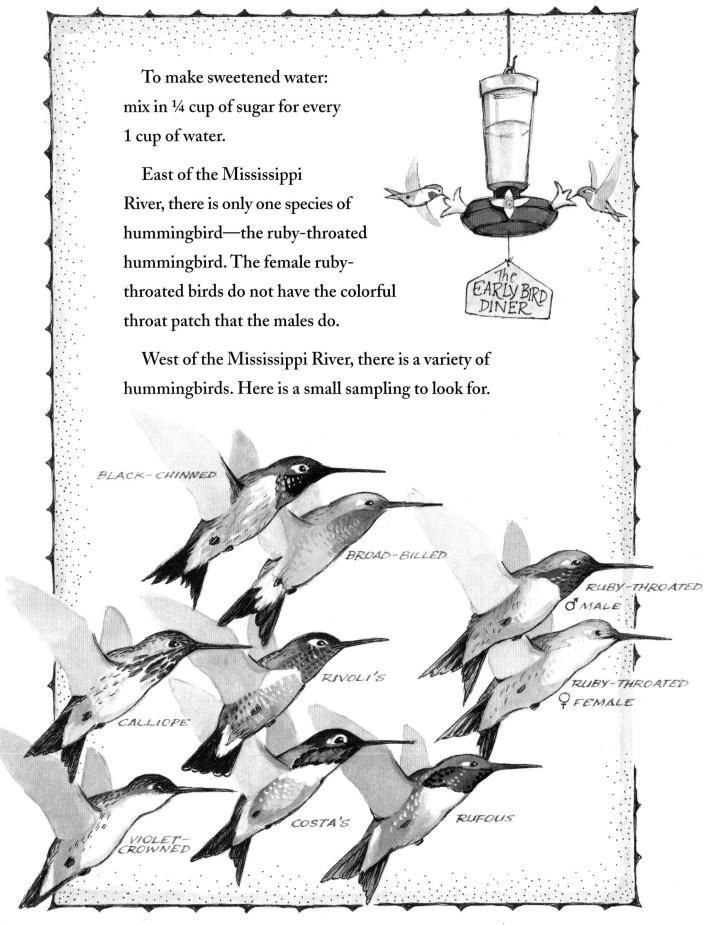

I love trees! Trees shade and cool the earth. Their roots hold soil in place so it doesn't wash away with the rains. Tree leaves produce oxygen for the air we breathe. And tree trunks, limbs, and branches create high safe havens for wildlife.

Sometimes giving back to Nature means
helping it regrow. For every tree that falls
from age or an ax, heavy snow or strong winds
blowing, I plant one to take its place and keep
the forest growing.

Every tree starts off as a tiny seedling. Even
this massive oak tree was once small enough to
hold in the palm of your hand.

Plant a tree and watch it grow! All you need is
a shovel for digging, a container of freshwater, a
nursery seedling, and a sunny spot.

Tree roots probe the soil to find moisture and
nutrients. Some types of trees have shallow roots
that spread out underground. Others have long
taproots that dig deep down in the ground.

SHALLOW ROOTS

TAPROOT

Dig a hole just deep enough to fit all of the seedling's roots.

Gently refill the hole, covering the roots.

Pour about a glass full of water around the base of the seedling.

Water once a day for a week, then let the rains take over.

Sometimes giving back to Nature means respecting an animal's space. For big animals like deer, moose, bears, and wolves, I give them space to hunt for food, space to run, and space to raise their young.

The space an animal needs to be healthy in the wild is called its home range. One animal's home range can overlap many other animals' home ranges, and may even include parts of your neighborhood.

Some large animals live within a surprisingly small home range. White-tailed deer live their entire lives in less than one square mile of woods and fields.

Other animals need more space to roam. A black bear's home range is 10 to 40 square miles, depending on the availability of food.

A timber wolf's home range covers 100 or more square miles. A mountain lion's home range can be anywhere from 20 to 40 square miles.

Here are some other animals' home ranges:

Red fox—1 square mile

Bobcat—6 square miles

Raccoon—6 to 10 square miles

Moose—3 to 4 square miles

The next time you see a wild animal, think about its home range. Where does it run and play and sleep? Where does it find food and water?

Animals come to this brook to drink the cold, clear water. I help keep the water cold by planting trees on the stream bank for shade. By picking up fallen branches, rotting leaves, and other litter near or in the stream, I help keep the water clean.

Sometimes giving back to Nature means picking up after yourself. Trash in a stream can be harmful to wildlife.

If you fish, wind your broken line into a small, neat wad and take it away with you. Animals can become tangled in discarded fishing line. Also, be sure to use only non-lead sinkers. Lost lead sinkers are toxic to fish that may accidentally swallow them.

LEAD SINKER

The plastic rings of drink holders can strangle small animals. Always cut or break the rings before throwing the holders in the trash.

I like to cool my bare toes in the water. But when I'm walking in a shallow stream, I wear thick-soled water shoes to protect my feet from sharp stones.

When I leave the stream, I scrub my water shoes clean to avoid spreading unwanted waterweeds or algae from one stream to another.

By caring for this little brook that runs right by my home, I'm taking care of water wherever water roams. Small streams like this feed the rivers that flow into the sea.

Clean freshwater is a gift I'm giving to the sea.

No one can say exactly how long it takes for freshwater from a mountain brook or inland river to reach the salty sea. But when it arrives, it won't be clean if no one cares along the way.

Where freshwater mixes with salt water, fish spawn. Many large ocean fish begin life in smaller streams like this one. If you are fishing in a stream for food, always make sure to release a fish too small to eat.

How to Release a Fish Unharmed

1. Grasp the fish firmly, but do not squeeze. (Be careful of sharp fins or gill covers.)

2. Use pliers to remove the hook.

3. Lower the unhooked fish into the water and let it go.

4. If it doesn't swim right away, push it forward and backward to move water through its gills until it revives and swims away.

(For fish with stingers, such as rays and skates, simply cut the line and let them swim away. The fishhook will eventually corrode and fall away.)

MUS   UASH III

Sometimes giving back to Nature means leaving things where you found them. When you wade in the ocean, you are walking on the edge of a vast underwater wilderness. You never know what might wash up with the next wave.

Bring home only empty shells. Here are some ways to tell if a seashell still has an animal living inside.

Conchs and whelks are gastropods, named for the way they appear to move along on their bellies. Any gastropod shell that feels heavy is still occupied. Put it back exactly where you found it. The animal was on its way somewhere when you picked it up.

GASTROPOD

Empty shark and ray egg cases feel dried and hard and are feather light in your hand.

SHARK EGG CASE

BIVALVE

Mussels, clams, and scallops are all bivalves. Each has two shells that open and close to catch food. A bivalve that is tightly closed is still alive. Return it to the water.

Sometimes giving back to Nature means simply protecting it. Sand dunes protect salt marshes and coastal homes from the ocean's pounding waves. The roots of grasses and other dune plants hold the sand dunes together and anchor them in place when storm winds and waves hit. Without the plants, the dunes would slowly wash away.

Walking or running on sand dunes destroys dune plants. To protect dune plants, always walk around a sand dune or follow an established path or boardwalk. That way, the dunes can go on protecting the coast.

MONARCH CATERPILLAR

When you leave the beach after a long day of playing, there are many creatures that come out in the dark.

If you like to catch caterpillars, lightning bugs, frogs, or salamanders to look at and admire up close, don't keep them longer than fifteen minutes and, if possible, release them exactly where you found them.

LIGHTNING BUG

WOOD FROG

SPOTTED SALAMANDER

Sea turtles are at home in the water, where they are weightless and swim swiftly and freely. They feel less at home on shore, where they must crawl slowly to lay their eggs in the sand. If you live on a beach where turtles nest, don't disturb them by coming too close. Don't shine any light on them. Keep beachfront porch lights turned off. The turtles will feel safer and more at home in the dark.

Every creature is happiest at home, where the sights and sounds and smells are most familiar.

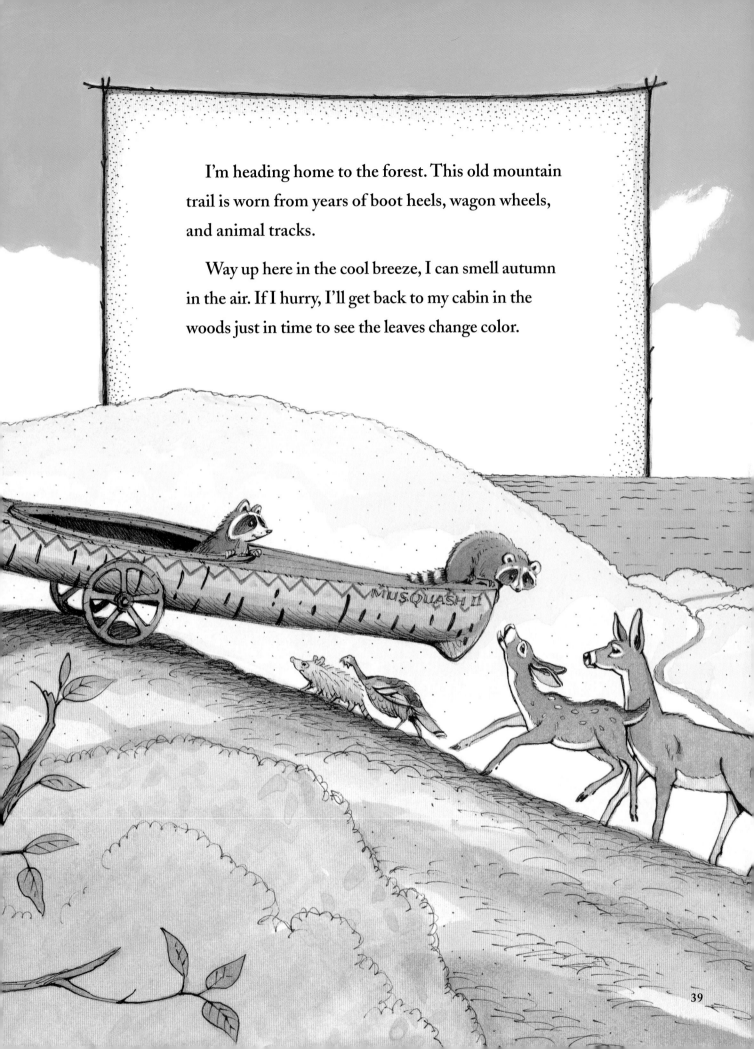

I'm heading home to the forest. This old mountain trail is worn from years of boot heels, wagon wheels, and animal tracks.

Way up here in the cool breeze, I can smell autumn in the air. If I hurry, I'll get back to my cabin in the woods just in time to see the leaves change color.

Sometimes giving back to Nature means learning new ways of doing things, like composting autumn leaves instead of burning them or throwing them in the trash. Composting means letting biodegradable things such as grass clippings or leaves break down and decay naturally.

The simplest way to compost the leaves you rake is to spread them onto your garden or yard. The leaves you scatter will eventually decompose and turn into fertilizer for the soil.

Some communities have a collection center where you can drop off bags of grass clippings and leaves to be composted.

As the first flurries of snow start to float down, it's time to think about keeping warm and conserving energy so we'll have enough to last all winter. I have my warm woolly sweater and just enough firewood to heat my tiny house.

You can give back to Nature by conserving energy in your home.

- Use energy-saving lightbulbs.
- Turn off lights when you leave a room.
- Shut off your TV and computer when you're not using them.
- Never leave a water faucet running or dripping.
- Always close the door when you come in from the cold.

If everybody does these things, it will save a lot of energy. The more energy we save, the less we take from Nature.

In winter, wild animals that don't hibernate or migrate to warmer places must conserve energy too. They do this by moving only when they have to find food or escape danger.

Never let your pets run free outdoors in winter. Outside, a house cat can prevent a bird from flying to food or keep a hungry mouse or squirrel from coming out to feed. And a playful pet dog may chase rabbits or deer, forcing them to use up precious energy needed to stay warm.

The Earth is our home. We breathe the air and drink the water. We use the land to grow our food. We live everywhere from the highlands and lowlands to the mountains and the sea. We like having wild places to explore. We love to fish and hike and swim. We watch and study wildlife and enjoy the great outdoors.

By giving back to Nature, we also help ourselves.

Remember: We're part of Nature too!

Answer key to page 9

Clockwise from upper left corner:
chickadee, evening grosbeak, goldfinch,
crossbill, cardinal, white-breasted
nuthatch, red-breasted nuthatch, brown
creeper, tufted titmouse, English sparrow,
downy woodpecker, turkey, blue jay,
mourning dove, crow, slate-colored
junco, hairy woodpecker, tree sparrow,
snow bunting, common redpoll, pileated
woodpecker, pine siskin, purple finch.